To: Chelsea
To: Matthew + Jamie
        Skinner
Sept, 27th 1995

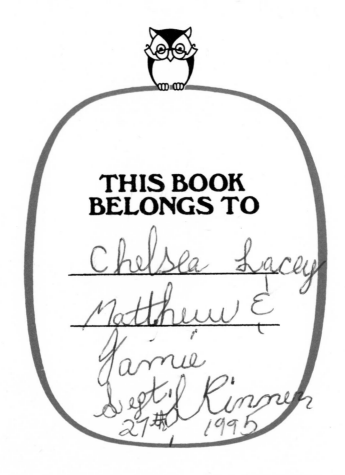

THIS BOOK
BELONGS TO

Chelsea Lacey
Matthew E
Jamie
Sept. L. Rinnen
27# 1995

Published in Great Britain by World International Publishing Limited.
A Pentos Company,
P. O Box 111, Great Ducie Street, Manchester M60 3BL.
Printed in Hungary. SBN 7235 4962 1

A LITTLE OWL BOOK
The Elves and The Shoemaker

retold by Hilda Young

illustrated by Susan Aspey

WORLD

There was once a shoemaker who, although he worked very hard all day long, was always poor. One night as he sat by candlelight cutting out his leather for a pair of shoes he said to his wife, "I have only enough leather to make one more pair of shoes. What is to become of us?"

He put the unmade shoes on his workbench, ready to start work on them the next day, and off they went to bed.

But the next morning there on his workbench stood a fine pair of shoes, neatly sewn, without one careless stitch. They were the grandest shoes the shoemaker and his wife had ever seen!

The shoemaker quickly put the shoes in the window of his shop, where they were seen and bought by an elegant gentleman who paid the shoemaker handsomely.

That evening the shoemaker left two pairs of dainty slippers cut out in soft leather, ready to be sewn . . . and next morning there they were, perfect in every detail.

He and his wife could hardly believe their eyes as they offered the slippers for sale.

Two fashionable young ladies bought them at once . . . and for the first time the shoemaker was able to buy both leather and food!

Times were now much happier for the kindly shoemaker and his wife. Whatever leather the shoemaker cut out and left on his workbench at sunset, was made up into shoes by daybreak. Soon the shoemaker's window was filled with every kind of shoe, each one soft, smart and very comfortable, obviously made by a master craftsman.

Customers came from miles around to buy the shoes. The shop doorbell never stopped ringing all day, as customers came in and out.

With the money they got for their shoes, the shoemaker and his wife were able to buy themselves new clothes and good wholesome food so that they never went hungry.

Christmas time drew near, and one evening, as the shoe-maker and his wife sat contentedly by their fire, he said, "Wife, I have a notion to stay up tonight and see if I can discover who it is who has helped us so kindly."

"Then I shall stay up with you," replied his wife, "for it is a thought I too have often had!"

So, as midnight approached, the couple left a candle burning in the room, and they hid behind a curtain from where they could watch without anyone discovering them.

Suddenly, on the stroke of midnight, two little elfin men ran into the room. They had neither coats to their backs nor shoes on their feet, but they quickly sat down at the shoe-maker's bench and started to work.

From their hiding place behind the curtain, the shoemaker and his wife watched in amazement as the elves took up the cut leather and began to stitch, sew and hammer, using their tiny fingers with amazing skill.

The little men worked on all through the night, not stopping until all the shoes had been finished. Then, as swiftly and as silently as they had appeared, they ran out of the room.

The shoemaker and his wife looked at each other. Then the shoemaker's wife spoke at last. "Husband," she cried, "now that we know who has helped *us*, we must help *them!* I will make them some clothes to keep them warm in the cold night air. And you shall make each of them a fine pair of shoes!"

"That is one task that I will most willingly undertake, wife!" cried the shoemaker.

All that day the shoemaker and his wife worked hard making their gifts for their elfin friends. The shoemaker made two tiny pairs of shoes, and his wife made each elf a shirt,

a coat and a waistcoat, and she even knitted them a pair of stockings!

They put the gifts on the workbench, and once again they hid behind the curtain as they heard the clock strike midnight.

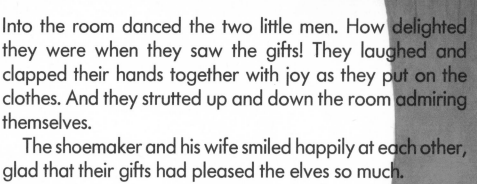

Into the room danced the two little men. How delighted they were when they saw the gifts! They laughed and clapped their hands together with joy as they put on the clothes. And they strutted up and down the room admiring themselves.

The shoemaker and his wife smiled happily at each other, glad that their gifts had pleased the elves so much.

But suddenly the elves cried:
"Thank you kindly for our clothes,
And these fine shoes upon our feet,
But now no longer need we work,
For we are both so smart and neat."

And away they danced, out of the lives of the shoemaker and his wife forever.

Yet although the shoemaker never saw the elves again, they left him the gift of good fortune. The shoemaker continued to make excellent shoes, his business prospered and he and his wife lived happily for the rest of their lives.